Jon Fosse was born in 1959 on the west coast of Norway. Since his 1983 fiction debut, *Raudt, svart* [Red, Black], Fosse has written prose, poetry, essays, short stories, children's books and over forty plays. In 2023, he was awarded the Nobel Prize in Literature 'for his innovative plays and prose which give voice to the unsayable'.

Damion Searls is a translator from German, Norwegian, French and Dutch, and a writer in English. He has translated nine books by Jon Fosse, including the three books of *Septology*.

T0326105

less than a desperate prayer made radiant by sudden spikes of ecstatic beauty.'
— Lauren Groff, *Literary Hub*

'*Septology* is the only novel I have read that has made me believe in the reality of the divine, as the fourteenth-century theologian Meister Eckhart, whom Fosse has read intently, describes it: "It is in darkness that one finds the light, so when we are in sorrow, then this light is nearest of all to us." None of the comparisons to other writers seem right. Bernhard? Too aggressive. Beckett? Too controlling. Ibsen? "He is the most destructive writer I know," Fosse claims. "I feel that there's a kind of – I don't know if it's a good English word – but a kind of reconciliation in my writing. Or, to use the Catholic or Christian word, peace."'
— Merve Emre, *New Yorker*

'Fosse's fusing of the commonplace and the existential, together with his dramatic forays into the past, make for a relentlessly consuming work: *Septology* feels momentous.'
— Catherine Taylor, *Guardian*

'A deeply moving experience. At times while reading the first two books of *Septology*, I walked around in a fugue-like state, wondering what it was that I was reading, exactly. A parable? A gospel? A novel bereft of the usual markings of plot, time, and character? The answer appeared to be all of the above... I hesitate to compare the experience of reading these works to the act of meditation. But that is the closest I can come to describing how something in the critical self is shed in the process of reading Fosse, only to be replaced by something more primal. A mood. An atmosphere. The sound of words moving on a page.'
— Ruth Margalit, *New York Review of Books*

'Having read the Norwegian writer Jon Fosse's *Septology*, an extraordinary seven-novel sequence about an old man's recursive reckoning with the braided realities of God, art, identity, family life and human life itself, I've come into awe and reverence myself for idiosyncratic forms of immense metaphysical fortitude.'
— Randy Boyagoda, *New York Times*

'[P]alpable in this book is the way that the writing is meant to replicate the pulse and repetitive phrasing of liturgical prayer. Asle is a Catholic convert and, in Damion Searls's liquid translation, his thoughts are rendered in long run-on sentences whose metronomic cadences conjure the intake and outtake of breath, or the reflexive motions of fingers telling a rosary. These unique books ask you to engage with the senses rather than the mind, and their aim is to bring about the momentary dissolution of the self.'
— Sam Sacks, *Wall Street Journal*

'The entire septet seems to take place in a state of limbo... Though Fosse has largely done away with punctuation altogether, opting instead for sudden line breaks, his dense, sinuous prose is never convoluted, and its effect is mesmerizing.'
— Johanne Elster Hanson, *TLS*

'Fosse has written a strange mystical moebius strip of a novel, in which an artist struggles with faith and loneliness, and watches himself, or versions of himself, fall away into the lower depths. The social world seems distant and foggy in this profound, existential narrative, which... promises to be a major work of Scandinavian fiction.'
— Hari Kunzru, author of *White Tears*

'The reader... is both on the riverbank and in the water being carried forward, and around, by the great, shaping, and completely engrossing, flow of Fosse's words. It's a doubleness of view that is reflected in the characters, named Asle, who are both one and other, and through which we can see and feel the world, and ourselves, more clearly.'
— David Hayden, author of *Darker with the Lights On*

'The translation by Damion Searls is deserving of special recognition. His rendering of this remarkable single run-on sentence over three volumes is flawless. The rhythms, the shifts in pace, the nuances in tone are all conveyed with masterful understatement. The *Septology* series is among the highlights of my reading life.'
— Rónán Hession, *Irish Times*

'Beautifully and movingly strange.... With *Septology*, Fosse has found a new approach to writing fiction, different from what he has written before and – it is strange to say, as the novel enters its fifth century – different from what has been written before. *Septology* feels new.'
— Wyatt Mason, *Harper's*

'Fosse intuitively — and with great artistry — conveys ... a sense of wonder at the unfathomable miracle of life, even in its bleakest and loneliest moments.... As the final pages draw to their profound and breath-snatching close, *Septology* also attains that original ambition: it imbues the very enigma of life, which can seem at times so terrifyingly dark, with a light that is almost beatific.'
— Bryan Karetnyk, *Financial Times*

Fitzcarraldo Editions
8-12 Creekside
London, SE8 3DX
Great Britain

ISBN 978-1-80427-102-5

Design by Ray O'Meara
Typeset in Fitzcarraldo
Printed and bound by CPI Group (UK) Ltd

fitzcarraldoeditions.com

Aliss at the Fire
Jon Fosse
tr. Damion Searls

I see Signe lying there on the bench in the room and she's looking at all the usual things, the old table, the stove, the woodbox, the old panelling on the walls, the big window facing out onto the fjord, she looks at it all without seeing it and everything is as it was before, nothing has changed, but still, everything's different, she thinks, because since he disappeared and stayed gone nothing is the same any more, she is just there without being there, the days come, the days go, nights come, nights go, and she goes along with them, moving slowly, without letting anything leave much of a trace or make much of a difference, and does she know what day it is today? she thinks, yes well it must be Thursday, and it's March, and the year is 2002, yes, she knows that much, but what the date is and so on, no, she doesn't get that far, and anyway why should she bother? what does it matter anyway? she thinks, no matter what she can still be safe and solid in herself, the way she was before he disappeared, but then it comes back to her, how he disappeared, that Tuesday, in late November, in 1979, and all at once she is back in the emptiness, she thinks, and she looks at the hall door and then it opens and then she sees herself come in and shut the door behind her and then she sees herself walk into the room, stop and stand there and look at the window and then she sees herself see him standing in front of the window and she sees, standing there in the room, that he is standing and looking out into the darkness, with his long black hair, and in his black sweater, the sweater she knit herself and that he almost always wears when it's cold, he is standing there, she thinks, and he is almost at one with the darkness outside, she thinks, yes he is so at one with the darkness that when she opened the door and looked in she didn't notice at first that he was standing there, even though she knew, without thinking it, without saying it

9

to herself, she knew in a way that he'd be standing there like that, she thinks, and that his black sweater and the darkness outside the window would be almost one, he is the darkness, the darkness is him, but still that's how it is, she thinks, it's almost as though when she came in and saw him standing there she saw something unexpected, and that's what's really strange, because he stands there like that all the time, there in front of the window, it's just that she usually doesn't see it, she thinks, or that she sees it but doesn't notice it somehow, because it's also that his standing there has become a kind of habit, like most anything else, it has become something that just is, around her, but now, this time, when she came into the room she saw him standing there, she saw his black hair, and then the black sweater, and now he just stands there and looks out into the darkness and why is he doing that? she thinks, why is he just standing there like that? if there was anything to see out the window now she could probably understand it but there isn't anything to see, nothing, just darkness, this heavy almost black darkness, and then, maybe, a car might come by, and then the light from the car's headlights might light up a stretch of the road, but then again not many cars come driving by and that's just how she wanted it, she wanted to live somewhere where no one else lived, where she and he, Signe and Asle, were as alone as possible, somewhere everyone else had left, somewhere where spring is spring, autumn is autumn, winter is winter, where summer is summer, she wanted to live somewhere like that, she thinks, but now, when the only thing to see is darkness, why would he just stand there looking out into the darkness? why does he do that? why does he just stand there like that all the time, when there's nothing to see? she thinks, and if only it was spring now, she thinks, if only spring would come now, with its light, with warmer days, with little flowers in the meadows, with trees putting out buds, and leaves, because this darkness, this endless darkness all the time now, she can't stand it, she thinks, and she has to say something to him, something, she thinks, and then it's as if nothing is what it was, she thinks, and she looks around the room and yes everything is what it was, nothing is different, why does she think that, that something is different? she thinks, why should anything be different? why would she think something like that? that anything could really be different? she thinks, because there he is standing in front of the window, almost impossible to separate from the darkness outside, but what has been wrong with him lately? has something happened? has he changed? why has he gotten so quiet? but, yes, quiet, yes, he was always a quiet type, she thinks, whatever else you can say about him he's always been quiet, so that's nothing out of the ordinary after all, it's, it's just how he is, that's just the way he acts, that's just how it is, she thinks, and now if only he could turn around and face her, just say something to her, she thinks, anything, just say anything, but he keeps standing there as if he never even noticed her come in

There you are, Signe says

and he turns to her and she sees that the darkness is also in his eyes

I guess I am, yes, Asle says

There's not much to look at out there, Signe says

No nothing, Asle says

and he smiles at her

No just darkness, Signe says

Just darkness yes, Asle says

Then what are you looking at, Signe says

I don't know what I'm looking at, Asle says

But you're standing there in front of the window, Signe

says
I am, Asle says
But you're not looking at anything, Signe says
No, Asle says
But why are you standing there then, Signe says
Yes I mean, she says
Yes are you thinking about something, she says
I'm not thinking about anything, Asle says
But what are you looking at, Signe says
I'm not looking at anything, Asle says
You don't know, Signe says
No, Asle says
You're just standing there, Signe says
Yes I'm just standing here, Asle says
Yes you are, Signe says
Does it bother you, Asle says
It's not that, Signe says
But why are you asking, Asle says
I was just asking, Signe says
Yes, Asle says
I didn't mean anything by it, I was just asking, Signe
says
Yes, Asle says
I'm just standing here, yes, he says
A lot of times when someone says something they
don't really mean anything by it, probably, he says
Probably almost never, he says
They just say something, just to say something, that's
true, Signe says
That's what it's like, yes, Asle says
They have to say something, Signe says
They have to, Asle says
That's how it is, he says
and she sees him stand there and sort of not entirely

know what to do with himself and then he raises one hand and lowers it again and then he raises his other hand, holds it halfway in front of him, and then raises the first hand again

What are you thinking about, Signe says

No nothing special, Asle says

No, Signe says

I guess I, Asle says

Yes I, he says

and he stands there and he looks at her

I, he says

I, I, yes well, I'll just, he says

You, Signe says

Yes, Asle says

You'll, Signe says

I, Asle says

I guess I'll go out onto the fjord for a while, he says

Today too, Signe says

I think so, Asle says

and he turns back to the window and again she sees him stand there and be almost impossible to separate from the darkness outside and again she sees his black hair in front of the window and she sees his sweater become one with the darkness outside

Today too, Signe says

and he doesn't answer and today he'll row out onto the fjord again, she thinks, but the wind is really blowing, and it probably won't be long before it starts to rain, but does he care about that, whatever the weather is he goes out in his little boat, a small rowboat, a wooden boat, she thinks, and what's so nice about rowing out on the fjord in a little boat like that? it must be freezing cold, and the fjord just there, with its water, its waves, maybe there might be something nice about it in the summer, rowing out on the fjord when the fjord is sparkling blue, when it glitters all blue, then maybe it's tempting, when the sun is shining on the fjord and the water is calm and everything is blue upon blue, but now, in darkest autumn, when the fjord is grey and black and colourless and it's cold and the waves are high and rough, not to mention in winter when there's snow and ice on the seats of the boat and you have to kick at the rigging to get it loose, get it free of the ice, if you want to free the boat from its moorings, and when snow-covered ice floes are floating on the fjord, why then? what's the appeal of the fjord then? no she just doesn't understand it, she thinks, to put it bluntly, she thinks, she doesn't get it at all, it is a total mystery to her, and if it was only every now and then that he went out onto the fjord, to fish maybe, to set out nets or something, but no, every single day he rows out onto the fjord, sometimes twice a day, in the dark, in the rain, in rough water, every month of the year, does he not want to be with her? is that why he always wants to go out onto the fjord? she thinks, what other reason could there be really? and hasn't he changed recently, he is so rarely happy now, almost never, and he is so shy, he really is, he doesn't want to see people and he turns away if anyone does come and if it ever happens that he does have to talk to someone he stands there and doesn't know what to do with his hands, doesn't know what to say, he stands there and feels sick with embarrassment, everybody can see it, she thinks, and what is the matter with him? she thinks, he was always a little like that, a little withdrawn, a little as if he thought of himself as always being a lot of trouble for other people, as upsetting other people just by being there, as a nuisance, an obstacle to what this or that other person wanted, as if he didn't understand, and it's getting worse and worse, before he could at least be around other people but now not any more, now he goes off to be by himself the second anyone other than her appears

You're going out onto the fjord, that's what you're thinking, Signe says

I'm not thinking anything, Asle says

Not thinking anything, Signe says

No, Asle says

I'm not thinking anything, he says

I'm just standing here, he says

You're just standing there, Signe says

Yes, Asle says

What day is it today, Signe says

Tuesday, Asle says

It's a Tuesday in late November in 1979, he says

The year's going by fast, Signe says

Unbelievably fast, Asle says

It's a Tuesday in late November, Signe says

Yes, Asle says

and he steps away from the window and he goes to the hall door

You're going, Signe says

Yes, Asle says

Where, Signe says

Just out for a while, Asle says

Yes well no one's stopping you, Signe says

Yes, Asle says

and she sees him go over to the stove, he takes a log and he bends down and he puts the log in the stove and then he stands up and looks at the flames and he stays standing like that for a while and looks at the flames before he goes over to the hall door and she sees his hand on the door handle, as though with a small hesitation, a lingering, and should she say something? or is it he who should say something? but neither of them has anything to say and then he pushes the handle down

There isn't something you're, says Signe

No no, says Asle

and he pulls the door towards him, goes out, and it is as if he wants to turn to her and say something to her, but he just shuts the door behind him, she thinks, and there is nothing to say, and he just opened the door and walked out, she thinks, but then again there are no problems between them, everything is good, they really are the closest couple you can imagine, the two of them, they never say anything to hurt each other, and he probably doesn't even know, she thinks, what good he can do for her, he can be so unsure of himself, not knowing what he should say or do, but there's not any resentment of her in him, she's certainly never noticed any, she thinks, but then why would he want to be out on the fjord all the time? in that little boat he got himself, a little wooden boat, a rowboat, she thinks and she sees, lying there on the bench, herself standing there in the middle of the floor in the room and then she sees herself go over to the window and stand there and look out and now there is a little light outside, she thinks, standing there in front of the window, now it has got as light as it can probably get at this time of year, it's brightened up so much that you can see the sky in its grey and black, and the pale grey mountain on the other side of the fjord, now you can see that too, she thinks, but down below on the big road, what's that gleaming there? who's that standing there? who's that? and who are the people walking there? is it she herself standing down there? and does she look scared? desperate? as though she is dissolved and in the process of disappearing altogether? does she really look like that? she thinks, who is that? she thinks, but no, she is standing right here, in front of the window, she is standing here and looking out,

16

so why did she get it into her head that she was standing down there on the big road, as though dissolved? why see something like that and think something like that? no it can't be, she thinks, because she's standing here, here in front of the window, and she's looking out, but she can't stay standing like this, here in front of the window, after all she stands here so much, she just stands like this almost all the time, stands and looks out the window, and sometimes she looks down at the big road, sometimes at the little road, that's what they called it, she thinks, the little road, to go with the big road, it was supposed to sound kind of cute, or maybe it was just to have a name for the road, and so it stayed the little road, that's what they called it, the road that went down to the big road from the old house, their home, where they live, the old house, the oldest parts of the house are several hundred years old, and then it was added onto, here and there, and she herself has lived here for more than twenty years now, no, such a long time? can it really have been so long? she thinks, and so it must be twenty-five years or so since she met him for the first time, since she saw him come walking up to her, with his long black hair, and there and then, it was really like that, there and then it was basically certain that he and she would be together, it was really like that, she thinks and she looks out at the big road winding there along the fjord, a thin line, and she can't see him anywhere, she thinks, and then she looks at the path that runs from the big road down to the bay and the boat-house, and to the landing, and then she looks at the fjord lying there, always the same, always changing, and then she looks at the mountain on the other side of the fjord, so steep, plunging straight down somewhere between black and grey from the sky's light movements that are some-where between grey and white, down to the line of trees edging the fjord, and now the trees are black too, and it would be so nice if they were green again, shining green, she thinks and she looks at the mountain again, and, she thinks, it is as if the mountain down there was breathing out, no she really has to stop it now, thinking something like that, the mountain breathing out, that doesn't make any sense, a mountain exhaling, she thinks, but still it is sort of like that, like the mountain was exhaling out there as it fell further and further down to the place where the trees start and then foothills and meadows, and houses, here and there a house scattered around, and the places where a couple of houses are standing right next to each other, and down on the fjord she can see the narrow stripes, that one is the big road winding back and forth, almost down to the landing, and then back up away from the fjord, further on, before it winds around the fjord, worn out and exhausted, and disappears for good, that's how it is, and now it is almost all black, that's how it is now, in late autumn, and that's how it is all winter long, she thinks, but in spring, in summer, it's different then, then everything can be together like blue and shining green and then the sky and fjord can face each other and both will be the bluest blue, and both can glow on the headland, yes, that's how it was, and that's how it will be again, she thinks, but she can't stay standing in front of the window like this, she thinks, why does she do that all the time? and now she mustn't think what she has thought so many times before, that she might just as well do that as do anything else, she thinks, instead she stays standing and she looks at a place in the middle of the fjord and then she loses herself in looking out at that place and she sees, lying there on the bench, herself standing there in front of the window and he too, she thinks, he too stood there so many times, just like she now sees herself standing there,

18

he too stood there like that in front of the window, like she now sees herself standing, before he disappeared and stayed gone, gone forever, he often stood like that and looked and looked, and the darkness outside the window was black and he was almost impossible to tell apart from the darkness out there, or else the darkness out there was almost impossible to tell apart from him, that's how she remembers him, that's how it was, that's how he stood, and then he said something about how he wanted to go out on the water for a little while, she thinks, but she never, or almost never, went with him, the fjord was not for her, she thinks, and maybe she should have gone with him more often? and if she had been with him on that evening, then maybe it never would have happened? then maybe he would be here now? but she can't think like that, that won't get her anywhere, she thinks, she never liked being out in a boat, never, but he liked it, he just rowed out onto the fjord as much as he could, all the time, every single day, often twice a day, she thinks, and that he would just stay gone, disappear, never come back, just be gone and that she would be left here, alone, since they had never had children, the two of them, him and her, it was just him and her, she thinks, he was here, and then he was gone, disappeared, he walked up to her, with his long black hair, she had never seen him before and then he just came walking up to her, and then, yes, then, well she did wait a little while, but then she ran to him, she thinks, and then she stayed with him, living in his house, she thinks, stayed together with him, for many years it was like that but then as suddenly as when he had once come walking up to her he went away from her and now it's been many years since she's seen him, no one sees him, he is just gone, he was there and he disappeared, went away, away forever, but what was it he said before he went out that day when he disappeared? what did he say before he left, did he say something? something about going out onto the fjord for a little while, maybe? that's what he always used to say, something about how he wanted to row out onto the fjord in his boat? maybe he said something like that, that he wanted to do a little fishing, maybe, something like that, he probably said something totally ordinary, something he said all the time, the usual words and sentences, the ones that always come up, what people always say, he probably just said that, she thinks and she looks at the window and she sees herself standing there in front of the window and looking out and then she sees herself walk across the room and she sees herself go and pick up a log, bend down and put it in the stove and then she sees herself stand back up and look at the hall door and it opens and then he is standing there in the doorway, and he comes into the room, lets the door close behind him

I, I'm going out onto the fjord for a while, Asle says

All right, Signe says

It's got a bit lighter out, Asle says

Yes it's probably as light as it's going to get these days, Signe says

Light enough to go out for a while, in any case, Asle says

Yes you don't need that much light either do you, Signe says

No, Asle says

So I'm going out for a while then, he says

Go ahead, Signe says

Since you never seem to get tired of rowing out in that boat of yours, she says

I get tired of it sometimes, Asle says

You do, Signe says

Yes, Asle says

But then why do you row out in your boat, you do it almost all the time, Signe says

I guess I just do it, Asle says

You just do it, Signe says

Yes, Asle says

You don't even really want to go out in the boat, Signe says

No, Asle says

But can't you just stay home then, Signe says

I could, Asle says

You could, Signe says

Maybe I like being out there in the boat, Asle says

and they both look down, both stand there and look down

You don't want to be here with me, that's why, Signe says

No it's not that, Asle says

But that boat of yours is so small, Signe says

I like it, Asle says

I've had it a long time, for years, it's a good boat, a nice wooden boat, you know, he says

Of course I know, Signe says

Actually no, it's a toothpick and it's dangerous, it seems to me, she says

I've seen much better boats, she says

I like this boat, Asle says

But couldn't you get yourself a bigger boat, a safer boat, Signe says

I don't want a new boat, Asle says

Why do you like this boat so much, Signe says

I knew the man who built it, and he built it for me, Asle says

He built boats his whole life, the man who built it, and

he built one for me, he says

I went and looked at the boat while he was building it, he says

Yes, Signe says

Yes you remember that, Asle says

That's how it was, Signe says

Johannes in the Bay built it, yes, Asle says

That was his name, yes, Signe says

Johannes in the Bay, everyone called him that, Asle says

And now it's been a couple years since he died, he says

The years go by so fast, don't they, he says

Johannes in the Bay built boats his whole life, and my boat was one of the last ones he built, he says

But didn't you ask to have your boat built smaller than the boats he usually built, Signe says

Yes well, Asle says

A little smaller, he says

I wanted a boat that was a little smaller, he says

Why? Signe says

I thought it was nicer like that, Asle says

But then it probably isn't as stable as other boats, Signe says

No not entirely, Asle says

and she sees him go over to the hall door again

You're going, Signe says

and he stands and looks at her

Yes, Asle says

But, Signe says

Yes well you know, Asle says

Yes I'll just go out for a walk, the wind is too strong to row out onto the fjord today, he says

Sounds good, Signe says

Just a little walk, Asle says

Yes go for a little walk, go ahead, Signe says

The wind is terrible, and it's pretty dark, even now, when it's as light as it'll get all day, she says

Yes, Asle says

and she sees him go out the hall door and shut it behind him, and then she sees, lying there on the bench, herself walk through the kitchen door and she thinks that she lies here so much, either she lies here on the bench or she stands there in front of the window, the same as she did when he was still here too, and so why does she always have to see him walking in the door to the room? and why does she always have to see herself step away from the window and into the room and stop right there in the middle of the floor? why does she always have to see herself stand there and say something to him? and why does she always have to hear what he says? what she says? why is it like that? why is he still here? because he's gone, he's been gone for years, it's been years since he disappeared, but it's still as if he's still here, she sees the hall door open, she sees him stand there in the doorway, she sees him walk into the room, hears him say what he's said so many times before, that's how it is and that's how it will be even though he is gone forever, he is still always here, he is saying what he always said, he is walking the way he always walked, he is wearing the clothes he always wore, she thinks, and her, what about her? yes she just lies here on the bench or just stands there in front of the window and looks out the window the way she always stood and looked out, she thinks, yes, she stands there now the way she always did, or she lies here on the bench, she thinks and she sees herself walk in the door from the kitchen and she sees herself go over to the window and stand there in front of the window and she thinks, lying here on the bench, that she can't bear it, she doesn't understand it, she thinks, and why is it always like that? why is it as though he was still alive and was about to walk down the little road, the way he did so many times before he disappeared and was gone forever, even though it's been years and years since she's seen him walking down the little road, it's as though he was walking down the little road right now, she thinks and she sees herself stand there in front of the window and look out into the darkness, and there, there, she sees, she thinks standing there in front of the window, him walking down the little road and sees the old yellow-white cap he has on, and she's sure he's going to go row out onto the fjord anyway, she thinks and she turns around and looks at the bench and then she sees herself lying there on the bench, and it can't be! it can't! she is standing here in front of the window and then she sees herself lying there on the bench, and she looks so old lying there, so worn out, and her hair has all turned grey, but it's still long, and just think, to stand here in front of the window and look out and then to look over at the bench and then see herself lying there old and grey, she thinks, and she looks over to the stove and there, there on the chair next to the stove, she sees herself sitting there too! she thinks, not only does she see herself lying there old and grey on the bench but she also sees herself sitting there on the chair next to the stove, and she sits there knitting the black sweater he almost always wore, that he is wearing even now, she thinks and she sees that her hair is black and long and thick, where she's sitting, and there's a slight curl to her hair and she sits there and looks at the flames and her fingers keep knitting and knitting the black sweater he almost always wore and then she looks back at the bench and she sees herself lying there, and her hair has turned grey, but it's still long, lying there on the bench her hair has turned long and grey and she looks out the window and she sees him walk down the little road in the yellow-white cap he has just started wearing and she thinks that cap is horrible and he thinks he doesn't want to turn around now, if he turns around now he'll probably just see her standing there in the window, looking out the window, in the light from inside the room, she's standing, clearly visible, and looking out, so he doesn't want to turn around, he doesn't want to look in her direction, he just wants to go take a little walk out on the big road, it's not a good day to row out onto the fjord today, the wind is too strong, and there's not even any decent light out even though it's as light as it will get today, and soon the darkness will come down over everything again, he thinks, so he'd better stay on land today, he thinks, in any case that's what he had to tell her, he thinks, but anyway it's probably all right just to go out for a little walk, he thinks and he starts to walk down the big road and it's terrible how dark it is now, late in the autumn, they've already got to late November, it's a Tuesday in late November, in the year 1979, and even though it's only afternoon it has got as dark as if it was evening, that's how it is at this time of year, late in the autumn, he thinks, and after not much longer it will be just dark, dark all day, with no light left to speak of at all, he thinks, and it's good to go for a walk, he likes that, he thinks, it sometimes does take some effort to get out of the house, true, but as soon as you're out it's better, and he likes it, he likes to walk, he only needs to get going, to really get going, to find his own pace again, and then it's good, he thinks, it's as though the heaviness that otherwise fills his life gets a little lighter, it gets taken away from him, turned into movement, it leaves behind the heavy thick motionless blackness that life can be the rest of the time, he thinks, but when he's walking, he thinks, he can feel like a nice piece of old woodwork, yes well, how stupid! how stupid! he thinks, but he can feel like those beautiful boards in a nice old boat! no just think, thinking something so ridiculous, thinking something like that, to think that he could think he was like those nice boards in an old boat, he thinks, how can he even think something like that? he thinks, it's not right to think like that, that he's a board in a boat? no, how did he think that? he thinks and he looks up at the sky, and he sees that everything has got almost pitch black, and that now, it is only just afternoon, now everything has got so dark, he thinks, and it's a bit cold too, but he does have on his thick warm black sweater, he thinks, and he walks a little faster and he feels the darkness coming faster and faster too, the faster he walks the faster it gets dark, that's how it seems to him, he thinks, and is he getting a little cold? no, not that, he thinks, he has warm clothes on, after all he has on the black sweater she knit for him, the first winter she lived with him she knit him the sweater that he almost always wears when it's cold, it really keeps you warm, but why should he wear that sweater all the time? there's probably no reason, that's probably just the way it is, he thinks and he looks at the fjord and it's totally quiet, and the wind seems to be blowing a little less hard than it was a while ago, he thinks, so maybe he should still go out onto the fjord? and why does he always want to row out onto the fjord, all year round? he doesn't actually want to, he just does it, he thinks, he rows out onto the fjord, it doesn't matter what the weather is, good or bad, and why? to fish? yes, well, he does a little fishing, but it's been a long time since he was all that interested in fishing, so that can't be why, he thinks, no today he had better just take a walk, that's something he almost never does, he can't remember the last time he just took a walk down the big road, he thinks, and so why should he today? no, why think like that? why does everything need to have a reason? he thinks, now he should just take a little walk down the big road and then he should turn around and go home, to the old house, their home, to the house where he has lived his whole life, first with Father and Mother and his brothers and sisters and then with her, with the woman he married, and it's a nice old house, he thinks, and how old is it, no, nobody knows, but it's old, it is old, and it has stood where it's standing now for probably several hundred years, but why is the darkness coming so fast? suddenly it's almost totally dark? he thinks and he looks at the fjord and the waves are beating hard again on the shore and he can still see the waves, but mostly it's that he can hear them, he thinks, and now he needs to turn back, go home, and he doesn't really feel in the mood to go back home, and why doesn't he want to? is it her, is it that she is there and waiting for him, that she is standing there in the light of the window, is that what makes him not want to go back home? no it's not that either, but he is a little cold, and it's got almost dark now, just like that it's got dark, almost totally dark, so he should probably go home, he thinks, and he stays standing there and he looks at the shore, at the waves, and he looks out along the land, along the fjord, and he sees that the fjord and the mountain and the darkness are about to blend together, become one with each other, and now he has to go home, he thinks and he starts to go home, that was a short walk, he thinks, but he did get out for a little while anyway, he thinks, and now she must be waiting for him, she's always waiting for him, she's standing in the window, she's always standing there in the window, looking, waiting, he thinks and he walks further and when he's walked a little further, around the curve, he'll be able to look back home at the old house and see that there's a light in the window and see her standing in the window, he's sure of it, she is standing there in the light, in the window, framed by the darkness, and she is looking at him, even if she can't see him she's looking at him, and she sees him, and it's always like that, he thinks, and he walks out around the curve and he looks back home at the old house and there she stands, there in the light of the window she is standing and looking out into the darkness, and he knows that she sees him, she always sees him, he thinks and he wants to not look at the window, not look at her standing there, he thinks and he looks at the shore, and there, down there on the shore, down below the boathouse, a bonfire is burning there! no, that was strange, that doesn't make sense, he thinks, and then it's not strange, it's just how it should be, he thinks, because of course there should be a fire burning down on the shore in front of the boathouse, he thinks, there is nothing the least bit strange about it, he thinks, but then the fire is a lot closer to him than it was, it's practically right below him now, and not far away any more, not down below the boathouse on the shore, no now it's practically right here below him he thinks and he keeps walking, and he looks down, and now what's that? no that doesn't make sense, he thinks and he looks up and he sees that the fire is back on the shore below the boathouse again, back down on the bay, and then the fire gets smaller, turns into just a flame, flickering weakly in the wind and in the darkness and then he can see it in one place or another in the heavy darkness, and the darkness is as heavy as he is himself, he thinks, and the darkness is dense and thick, now it is one single darkness, a play of blackness, and then he can see a flicker of flame out there and then not any more, because then it's black, but then the flame is there again, and several flames, and then the flame gets bigger, it becomes a small fire again, out there, down in the bay, down below the boathouse a fire is burning now, he thinks, and he stops and he stands and looks at the fire. And now the fire is big. Down on the shore a fire is burning. And then the fire is near him again. And it must be the darkness, and the fact that he's so cold, that makes him unable to tell exactly where the fire is burning, he thinks, but he sees it, he does see it, there in the darkness, those yellow and red flames. And it looks warm, it looks good, because it's cold, yes, he thinks, it has got so cold that he has to keep walking, he can't stay standing in one place, it's too cold for that, he thinks and he starts to walk and he's freezing and it is so cold that he tries to walk as fast as he can and he can barely remember the last time it was so cold in the autumn, he thinks, it must have been back when he was young, because back then, or that's how he remembers it at least, it was almost always cold and there was ice on the fjord and so much snow on the hills, on the streets, ice and snow and cold, but now, in recent years, autumn has always been pretty mild, and then this year the cold set in again, he thinks, and he doesn't have a cap to wear any more, those old red knit caps with tassels from when he was a boy, you can't find them anywhere any more of course, and where did they go, and where do they come from anyway, caps like that? he thinks, they just disappear, the years go by and both the years and these red caps come from somewhere or another, he thinks, but then again, he thinks, he has finally found a cap, big and roomy, yellow-white, it must have been left behind by his Grandma, the one who was married to Olaf, his grandfather, Grandpa Olaf, who died when he himself was so little that he has no memory of him, Grandpa Olaf, but he definitely does remember, he thinks, that Grandma wore a cap like this, that has stuck with him, the way one thing or another can sometimes stick with you, yes he definitely remembers Grandma walking up to him in a cap like this and he also remembers the blue coat she wore and that she had a walking stick in her hand, he thinks, because it's slippery on the big road where Grandma comes walking up the hill and she has a walking stick in her hand so she can steady herself and keep on her feet and not fall down and break her bones, as she said, he thinks, and in her other hand is her shopping bag, a red bag, and on her head is the yellow-white wool cap that he himself always wears now, on these cold days. And is he going, he thinks, over to Grandma? Because he sees Grandma come walking up to him all right and he goes over to her

Grandma! Hi Grandma! Asle shouts

Have you been shopping, Grandma! he shouts

and Grandma smiles at him under her yellow-white cap, the one that he himself is wearing now, and she says he should just wait until she gets home, then he can see what she has

Come home with me, then you can see, Grandma says

I've gone shopping for a few things, I have, she says

and he sees that Grandma's bag is heavy

Should I help you carry it, Asle says

It's better if I do it myself, Grandma says

It's easier when I carry my own things, it's steadier walking like that, she says

But you could always take one handle of the shopping bag too and help me a little, that would be nice of you, she says

A little help is always good, she says

and he takes one handle of the shopping bag and then Grandma takes two fingers and puts them on top of his cold fingers and then they carry the shopping bag together, slowly, step by step, up the little road and neither of them says anything

You're a good boy, Asle, Grandma then says

and Grandma and he keep walking and he feels Grandma's cold and slightly stiff fingers on his fingers and he wants to pull his hand back, but he doesn't dare to, he thinks and he walks up the big road and now he has come to the flat place down below the house on the neighbouring farm, and can't he hear someone standing and talking in the yard there? does he hear that the two boys are talking there? or not? no it must have been nothing, he thinks and now he has to just go home, he thinks and he looks at the fire down there on the shore, and now the fire is big, and it's still hard to see if the fire is burning down on the bay below the boathouse or somewhere closer to him, he thinks, but it's big, the fire, and pretty, the yellow and red flames in the darkness, in this cold, and in the light from the fire he sees the waves of the fjord beat like always against the stones of the shore, or he doesn't see the waves, he thinks, he just sees the water coming in over the stones and running back out from the stones, the water moves in and out, it wets the stones and pulls back, he thinks and he stands there and stays standing and looking at the wet stones there in the light from the fire and then he looks at the fire and there in the fire, isn't that a body there in the fire? a person? he thinks, there in the middle of the fire he sees a bearded face and then the beard, it is grey and black both, starts to burn, and the long grey and black hair is also on fire and he sees staring eyes right in the middle of the fire and something in the eyes is as if sucked up by the flames and as if dispersed into the cold air as smoke and he sees eyes and he can't see the faces, they aren't faces, they're just grimaces, and he can't see the bodies, and then he sees the eyes sort of find a voice and what he hears is like a howl, first a howling from one eye

31

and then a scattered howling from lots of eyes and then the huge howl becomes one with the flames rising up and it disappears into the darkness and the voices in the eyes rise up and are smoke that you can't see and he keeps walking and now it's so cold that he has to go home, he thinks, it's too cold to stay out and even if their house is old it's warm there in the room back home in the old house, he thinks, they have a good stove, and they have a fire in it, and the wood is wood he got himself, in the summer he chops wood and in the autumn he saws up the wood to the proper length, splits it, stacks it so that it gets good and dry, he thinks, yes, they have wood, a good amount of wood, and it's good and warm, and before he went out he put a log in the stove, he thinks, and now she's probably put more wood in the stove, so that the fire wouldn't burn out, of course she has, so that it's warm enough and nice in the room at home in the old house, he thinks and he starts to walk up the little road back home to the old house and now he can't stop and look back down at the shore, now he has to go home, and he can't think again that he should go out onto the fjord for a while, it's too cold, it's dark, he can't think that, he thinks and he stops and he turns around and looks back down at the shore and there's still a fire, but it's smaller now, it's now just a little fire he sees burning down there on the shore, so is the fire already burned out, he thinks, or is that another fire? could that really be another fire? yes it must be another fire, he thinks, because the fire he saw before was so much bigger, it was really a huge fire, big and strong, but now he sees a little fire burning, he thinks and he looks back home, back at the old house, at the window, and there she is standing there, small, with her black hair, she is standing there looking out, she, his wife, she is standing there and looking out the window as though she was part of the window, she is standing there, he thinks, always, always, whenever he pictures her she is standing there in the window, maybe she didn't used to at first but lately, she has stood there all year lately, he thinks, that is how he remembers her, small, black hair, big eyes, and then the darkness like a frame around her, he thinks and he looks back down at the shore again and a little fire is burning steadily down on the shore, just below the boathouse, and then he sees, and even though it's dark he sees it as clearly as if it was bright daylight, a woman with a little boy she's carrying in her arm go up to the fire and in her other hand she is holding a plank of wood with bark on it that she lays on the fire and the woman stands there and looks into the flames, then she goes and picks up a stick with a sheep head on it, the stick goes in through the neck opening and the point of the stick comes out through the mouth, and she takes the stick over to the fire and she puts the stick with the sheep head on it into the flames and while the boy dangles in her arm she moves the sheep head back and forth in the flames, and then its wool catches fire and blazes up and then a burnt smell goes up, burning, and then she dips the sheep head into the water of the fjord before she puts it back into the flames, and again that burnt smell, and then she moves the sheep head back and forth, back and forth in the flames. That's Aliss, he thinks, and he sees it, he knows it. That's Aliss at the fire. That is Aliss, he thinks, his great-great-grandmother, he is sure of it. It's Aliss, he was named after her, or rather after her grandson Asle, the one who died when he was seven, the one who drowned, he drowned in the bay, his Grandpa Olaf's brother, his namesake. But that is Aliss, in her early twenties, he thinks. And the boy, about two years old, that's Kristoffer, his great-grandfather, the one who would later be Grandpa Olaf's father and also the father of the Asle he was named after, his namesake, the one who drowned when he was just seven years old, he thinks and he sees Kristoffer start to cry dangling there in Aliss's arm and she puts down the stick with the sheep head on it and then she sets Kristoffer down on the shore and he stands up and stands there unsteady on his little legs, and then Kristoffer takes one careful step, and he stands, and then he takes another step, and then he falls on his side and shrieks and Aliss says no, why do you have to try to stand up, can't you sit quiet, Aliss says, and she puts down the stick and she picks up Kristoffer and holds him tight to her chest

You good little boy, you're a good little boy, Aliss says

Don't cry now, don't cry any more, that's a good boy, she says

and Kristoffer stops crying, gives a little sob, and then he's happy again and then Aliss puts him down on the same stone as before and she picks up the stick with the sheep head again and starts to burn it, moves it back and forth in the flames. And again Kristoffer stands up. And again he takes a careful step forward. And then another. And Aliss stands there, moving the stick with the sheep head on it back and forth in the flames. That is Aliss. That's Aliss at the fire, he thinks and he sees Aliss standing there with her thick black hair, on her short legs, with her narrow hips. It's Aliss. She was my great-grandfather's mother, Kristoffer's mother, Kristoffer whose sons were Grandpa Olaf and Asle, the one I was named after, the one who drowned when he was only seven, who got a nice little boat for his seventh birthday and drowned on the same day, playing with the boat, down on the bay, he thinks and he sees Kristoffer toddle forwards, and it happens so slowly, he puts one foot in front of the other, stands there for a minute, then he takes the next step, forward, swaying back and forth a little, but forward, and then Kristoffer is standing in front of a pile of sheep heads and he feels the mouth of one of the sheep heads with his finger and then he slowly sticks his finger into a nostril and then quickly pulls his hand back again and then he stands there and looks at the sheep head, he looks into one eye, and then puts his finger right on the eye, feels it and then jerks back his finger very fast and again Kristoffer stands there and looks into the eye and again he puts his finger right on the eye and he presses his finger against the eyelid and then he pulls it down over the eye. And then Kristoffer stands there and looks at the eye. And Aliss turns around and walks over to Kristoffer waving the burned sheep head on the stick and she says do you really want to sit there and look at those woolly bloody sheep heads, you're not the one who has to, Aliss says, and she goes over to a trough and she uses the edge of the trough to pull the sheep head off the stick and then Aliss goes over to the pile of sheep heads and she drives the point of the stick into the neck opening of the sheep head that Kristoffer just pulled down the eyelid of and she pushes in the stick and then she picks up the sheep head and goes back over to the fire and puts the sheep head into the flame and the sharp smell spreads out and Aliss says no that doesn't smell very good my good little boy, she says, and she puts the sheep head with the burning wool into the water down off the side of the pier and then it sizzles and Kristoffer is startled and he looks scared and he looks at the sheep heads lying there in front of him and he sees that they're lying there quietly like before and he puts his finger into an open mouth and then quickly touches a tongue, then he grabs the teeth

No leave the sheep head alone now, Aliss says

They're not for poking and playing with, she says

Be a good boy, she says

and Kristoffer pulls back his hand and he looks at Aliss and then Kristoffer sees the pretty brown almost black boat lying there, in the middle of all that blue, and then he takes a step, and another, out on the pier, and then he goes further and he looks at the boat, black and pretty in the blue water, and Kristoffer is almost running out on the pier and then he is at the edge of the pier and he takes another step and he is there in empty space and then he is there in the water

Kristoffer, God save you! Aliss screams

and Aliss lets the sheep head be and lets the stick be and she is on the pier and she lies down flat on the edge of the pier and she stretches out her arm and she feels around in the water finds one of Kristoffer's feet and grabs it and pulls the foot towards her and then she finds an arm and she pulls Kristoffer up over the edge of the pier

No you've really done it now, Aliss says

I look away for a second and you run right into the water, she says

You can't be trusted, she says

No how could that happen, she says

and Aliss picks up Kristoffer, who suddenly starts shrieking with all his might, and she presses him to her breast, and then she hurries over to the boathouse

It's so cold in that water, yes, we need to get you inside so you can warm up, Aliss says

You can't catch cold on me, you good little boy, she says

My best little boy, you can't get sick and go away from your mama now, no, she says

You're my best little boy, Kristoffer, she says

and Aliss rubs Kristoffer's back and he has started to shake, shiver after shiver goes through his body

You can't freeze, and catch cold, Kristoffer, good boy,

Aliss says

No no, she says

Now you can't catch cold on me, you're a good boy, she says

and he sees, standing there on the little road, Aliss come up the hill towards him with Kristoffer pressed against her breast, she comes running, and with black hair thick around her face, and those big eyes, and Aliss is coming as fast as she can on her short legs, and then Kristoffer's terrified shrieking, and then this darkness, and these winds, and the rain, and now he has to get home soon, he thinks, because he can't just stay standing on the little road and not go into his own house, where he's lived his whole life, home into the old house, he thinks and he sees Aliss go past him and then he looks at her back, Aliss's back, his great-great-grandmother's back, that's her, that's Aliss, that's her he sees hurrying around the corner, with her black hair hanging far down her back, and with her narrow hips, her short thin legs. That's Aliss. That's his great-great-grandmother, probably around twenty years old, he thinks, and the boy she's pressing to her breast, about two years old probably, that's his great-grandfather, Kristoffer. And he goes around the corner too, and he looks at Aliss with Kristoffer pressed against her breast go home through the front door of the old house, and he sees the door shut and she sees, lying there on the bench, the hall door open and then she sees a small woman with long black hair come in, she has big eyes, she is carrying a boy pressed against her breast and the woman rushes across the room and then she puts the boy down next to her on the edge of the bench and then the woman pulls the boy's pants off, his sweater, she strips the boy totally naked and then she lays him down on the bench next to her, and the woman rubs his back again and again

There there, good boy, don't be cold any more, the woman says

Good boy Kristoffer, now you'll get all warm, the woman says

Don't freeze now, she says

Mama Aliss is here to rub you till you're all warm, you're a good boy, she says

and Aliss rubs Kristoffer all over his back again and again and she sees Aliss stand up and she looks at Kristoffer lying there next to her on the bench, and he is wet, he's sobbing a little, and there are shivers going through his body, and she sees Aliss go open the bedroom door and go in and then come back in and she is carrying a wool blanket and then Aliss comes over to the bench and she spreads the blanket out all over Kristoffer and then Aliss sits down on the edge of the bench and she starts to rub Kristoffer's back again, over and over, rubbing and rubbing his back

So, my darling Kristoffer, now you're getting warm again, good little Kristoffer, Aliss says

There there, good boy, good boy Kristoffer, she says

Just think, you fell in the water, such a little boy and you fell in the water, but luckily Mama Aliss was there, yes, she says

and she sees Aliss rub Kristoffer's back again and again and she looks at the window and she sees herself standing there looking out the window, and she's always standing there, why does she always have to stand there? there's no reason for her to stand there? she thinks and then she hears that Kristoffer is breathing evenly now and she sees Aliss stand up and go out the kitchen door and she looks at Kristoffer and then she puts her arms around him and then she hugs Kristoffer close and then she rubs and she rubs his back and then she lightly strokes his hair

and then she again sees herself standing there in front of
the window and looking out, and she has been standing
there so long now, almost motionless, she has stood there
in front of the window, she thinks and she thinks, standing there in front of the window, that now he really does
have to come home soon, why doesn't he come home?
and it's so cold out, windy, and raining, and why doesn't
he come home? she thinks, and there, out there in the
middle of the fjord, did she see something? no, nothing,
she probably just imagined it? she thinks, but now she
will probably have to go out soon and look for him, she
thinks, because she can't just stand here like this, in front
of the window, and he can't really have gone out in his
boat in this weather? or can he? no, he couldn't have, she
thinks, but there, down there on the shore, isn't that a fire
she sees there? no it can't be, on this dark evening, late in
November, in the rain and the wind, but still that really is
a fire she's seeing, isn't it? she thinks, it is, it's a fire, and
now she has to go look for him, whether she wants to or
not, she thinks and she turns around and she walks across
the room and she thinks that now she really will have to
go look for him soon and he thinks that he really has to
go inside soon, he thinks, standing there in the yard and
looking at the front step, big and broad, lying there heavy
in the light outside, and in this weather he can't just stay
standing around outside, he thinks, it's windy and raining, it is, and it's cold, too cold to stay outside, and what's
wrong with him? he thinks, why can't he just go inside?
what is it, why is he still waiting? what's stopping him?
what is it? he thinks and he opens the front door and the
doorknob is loose, two screws are missing and the other
three are loose, and he needs to fix that, he thinks, but it's
been like that for so long already, for years, he thinks, and
he has thought that he needed to fix it so many times, he

thinks, he thought it over and over again but it always just stays the way it is, he'll probably never do anything about it until the doorknob falls off and is lying on the front step, he thinks and he walks into the hall and the old walls there settle into place all around him and say something to him, the same way they always have, he thinks, it's always like that, whether he notices it and thinks about it or not the walls are there, and it is as if silent voices are speaking from them, as if a big tongue is there in the walls and this tongue is saying something that can never be said with words, he knows it, he thinks, and what it's saying is something behind the words that are usually said, something in the wall's tongue, he thinks, and he stands there and looks at the walls, no, what is wrong with him today? why is he being like this? he thinks, and he puts his hand flat on the wall, and it seems like the wall is telling him something, he thinks, something that can't be said but that is, just is, he thinks, and it's almost like he is touching a person, he thinks, almost like something is being said the way something is said when you touch someone, he thinks and he strokes the wall and there is almost a caress in his fingers running over the old brown panelling and then he hears footsteps and he pulls his hand back and then he sees the door from the room open and there she is standing in the doorway

It's good that you're home, Signe says

I, I was so worried about you, she says

Yes you know how I am, she says

and he says that he just went for a little walk out on the big road, that's all, he says and he looks down, looks up again at her standing there holding the door open, and she says he must not have gone out onto the fjord and he says no, not in this weather, it's too windy, and the rain, and it's dark too, he says

But you, Signe says

and the worry in her voice mixes with the silent calm in the wall's voice

Yes, Asle says

But you said you would, Signe says

I guess I did but I changed my mind, I just took a walk on the big road, Asle says

and she says that's good, since, yes, when the wind is blowing like it is now, and it's dark, and it's so cold, yes, he is likely to row out onto the fjord anyway, no matter what the weather is, he, she says, but it's cold and they shouldn't let the heat out of the room, she has warmed it up nicely, she says, so now he should come inside, she says

Well it's happened before, Asle says

What has, Signe says

Yes, that I said I'd go out for a while, that the wind was too strong and it was too dark to go out onto the fjord but that I did it anyway, Asle says

Yes that's happened before, you're right, Signe says

But not today, Asle says

It's good that you're home now, Signe says

and he stays standing there, he sort of doesn't quite know what to do with himself, he thinks

I, I was so worried about you, Signe says

What's the matter, she says

Now come inside, don't just stay standing there, she says

Yes, Asle says

and he looks at her gently

I'm coming right in, Asle says

and he stays standing there

But it's cold here, can't we go inside, there's a nice fire in the stove, Signe says

and then she goes and takes his hand lightly, and she

lets it go right away, and then she goes into the room and lying there on the bench she sees herself come into the room and then she sees him come in and she sees that right behind him Aliss comes in too, and she too walks into the room, and then she sees herself go over to the stove and pick up a log and she sees herself bend down and he looks at her standing there bending down in front of the stove and then she puts the log sideways in the flames and at the same time he sees that now it's Aliss who is putting a log in the stove, it's not her, it's Aliss, his great-great-grandmother, it's her standing in front of the stove now and putting a log sideways into the stove and it shines in her black hair and there on the bench, back there in the corner, he sees Kristoffer lying with a wool blanket wrapped around him and then he sees Aliss go over and sit down on the edge of the bench and she puts her hand on Kristoffer's forehead

You don't have a fever now do you, Kristoffer, do you, Aliss says

You feel a little warm, she says

Just go back to sleep, good boy, she says

and he sees Kristoffer nod and then he looks at her where she's standing in front of the stove and looking in at the flames

You're standing there and looking in at the flames, yes, Asle says

I guess I am, Signe says

and he sees that she stands there and looks in at the flames, and he sees that the flames gather around the wood and then fly up free of the wood, and then, very quickly, the wood has turned into part of the flames and he looks at the window and he looks at the flames reflected in the window and mixing with the darkness there outside and with the rain that's now running down over the window, and then he hears the wind

This wind is terrible, Signe says

Yes it seems to be picking up, Asle says

and he looks over at the bench and he sees Aliss lay down on the bench and put her arms around Kristoffer and she presses him to her, starts to rock him

These autumn storms are getting worse and worse, Asle says

These last few years it's just got worse, he says

But it's probably always like that, changing from year to year, he says

Anyway, it wasn't like this before, he says

and he goes over to the window and he stops in front of it and looks out and he says now it's blowing so hard that he's starting to get nervous about the boat, whether it's tied up tight, he says, maybe he should go out for a minute and check on the boat, he says and she says no, in this weather, do you really have to, she says, he surely must have tied the boat tight enough, she says and he says he probably did, and then the walls crack in the wind

Yes that was quite a gust, Signe says

Unbelievable how it's blowing, Asle says

I should really go check on the boat, he says

No do you really have to now, Signe says

It can't hurt, Asle says

But be careful then, Signe says

and he steps closer to the window and he tries to look out and he sees only the darkness and then the rain that covers the windowpane and then he says well I'll go then

Yes all right but come home again soon, Signe says

I'm just checking on the boat, Asle says

And I have good warm clothes on, he says

That's a good sweater you knit, he says

and he smiles at her and she sees him walk out the hall

door and shut it after him and she sees, lying there on the bench, herself standing in the middle of the room and why does she always have to see herself standing there? she thinks and she sees Aliss sit up on the edge of the bench and she pulls up her smock and then Aliss takes Kristoffer and lays him on her breast and he opens his mouth again and again and then he finds her nipple and then he sucks and sucks and she sees Aliss stroke his black hair and then she sees herself go over to the window and then she sees herself stop there in front of the window and look out and she thinks, lying there on the bench, why didn't he come back? what happened to him? why did he disappear, just stay gone, she thinks, he was always here, and then he just disappeared, and his boat, she thinks, was found floating in the middle of the fjord, empty, one dark autumn evening, in late November, years and years ago, twenty-three years it's been now, she thinks, 1979, a Tuesday, that's what happened, he never came back, and she thought that he was just staying out on the fjord a long time, she thinks, that he'd still come back, but the hours went by, hour after hour, no she can't bear to think about it, it's still so painful, she thinks, no she doesn't want to think about it, she thinks, because he's really just gone, he's never coming back, she went out to look for him, stood there on the pier, in the darkness, the rain, the wind, just stood there, and waited, now he'd have to come back soon? why isn't he coming? but he'll never, no she can't bear to think about it, come back, just the boat, it sat on the water of the bay and bumped against the stones on the shore, and the boat was empty, no she can't think about that, she thinks, he'll never come back, he disappeared, he's gone, they did look, yes, they looked for him, no, she can't bear to think about that, the search, several days looking, then the boat, empty, there on the shore, cast up on the shore by the waves, and then the two boys from the neighbouring farm who burned the boat, that was easy enough, she thinks, because the boat couldn't just stay lying there on the shore falling to pieces, and she didn't have the strength to do it herself, no the boat just lay there for maybe a year and then the two boys from the neighbouring farm came and asked if they could burn the boat for their Midsummer's Day fire, and of course they could, she thinks, and then the boys burned the boat, and then the boat was gone too, and she mustn't think about that, she can't bear it, she thinks, no she mustn't think about that, she can't bear it, she can't think about that, she thinks, and she never really fully understood him, not from the first time she met him, she thinks, and maybe that was why she felt so close to him, from the first time they saw each other, when he came walking up to her, with his long black hair, and from then on, and up until now, or in any case until he was gone, it had been the two of them, she thinks, and why was it like that? why? what ties two people together? or at least tied her to him, and he, well yes he was tied to her, him too, but maybe not quite as much as she was tied to him, but still, yes, yes, tied together, they were, of course they were, he to her, she to him, but maybe she was more tied to him than he was to her, that may well be, but does that mean anything? no why think something like that? she thinks, because he did stay with her after all, he didn't leave, he stayed here with her, right up until he just disappeared, she thinks, he was with her, from the first time she saw him come walking up, and then he looked at her, and she just stood there, and they looked at each other, smiled at each other, and it was as though they were old friends, as though they had always known each other, in a way, just that it had been such an immeasurably long time since they had last seen each other, and that's why they were so happy, to see each other again made them both so happy that happiness took over and steered them, it steered them to each other, as though this was something that was gone, that had been missing their whole lives, but now it was here, at last, it was here now, that's how it felt then, that first time they met, completely by accident, and it wasn't hard, it wasn't frightening, no, it was like it was obvious, like there was nothing to do about it, it was certain, somehow, and whether she said or did one thing or another it was kind of like it didn't make any difference, it happened the way it was meant to happen, it had all been decided in advance, she thinks, yes, yes that's how it was, there was nothing to do about it, but it took its time of course, he wasn't exactly a hothead after all, and she wasn't either, and they somehow didn't need to be either, it was there, and it was the way it was, whether they did anything or didn't do anything, she thinks, but eventually at some point there was a letter from him, a letter came, and he wrote how hard it had been to find out her address, wrote a little about day-to-day life, not much more than that, just a couple words, a few short ordinary words, no big words in any case, but it was enough, he didn't need anything more, and she answered, yes of course she did, and it was a little embarrassing to think about the letter she sent, she thinks, because even if he didn't really know what to make of big words she did, she wrote big words, but she can't think about that, because if there was one thing he didn't like it was big words, they just lied and covered things up, those big words, they didn't let what really was live and breathe but just carried it off into something that wanted to be big, that's what he thought, and that's how he was, he liked the things that didn't want to be big, she thinks, in life, in everything, and that's how it was with his boat too, a little wooden boat, a little row-boat, that this, this, Johannes, yes that was his name, the old man, this Johannes in the Bay had built, and you couldn't really trust either of them, the boatbuilder or the boat he built, and maybe, no she mustn't think that, she thinks and she sees herself standing there in front of the window and looking out and then she sees, lying there on the bench, Aliss take Kristoffer off her breast and he cries a little and then he falls asleep in Aliss's arms and then she sees Aliss pull her smock down and Aliss stands up with Kristoffer in her arms and she opens the door to the bedroom and then Aliss goes in and shuts the door behind her and then she looks at herself standing there in front of the window and looking out the window and now she can't stand here any more, she thinks, standing there in front of the window, she can't just stay standing here in front of the window, because he's not coming back, she has to do something, she has to sit down, put more wood in the stove, she can't stay standing here in any case, she thinks, because now he'll probably be home right away, she thinks, yes of course, the weather is too bad for him to stay out, and he can't just stay out on the fjord all night either, and if only you could trust that boat of his, because that boatbuilder, the old man, he was never entirely healthy, and how could you be if you spent your whole life standing there in a barn nailing boats together, nailing day in and day out until eventually there's a boat, a little wooden boat, a rowboat, fifteen feet long, maybe sixteen, and narrow, and pointed in front and in back, fore and aft, and thin, just a thin hull between the person sitting in the boat and the water, the waves, the depths of the fjord, the immeasurable depths, it's over three thousand feet from the surface, from here where there's light and darkness and air, down down down into the fjord until there is a kind of floor on the bottom. And then these thin planks of the boat, three to a side, between the man in the boat and the water and the great darkness below him, and then the waves, like the time she was with him in the boat and a wave crashed in over the side, no, no, she can't think about it, she thinks and she sees the rain running down the window, and she can't see anything out the window, just darkness, and then there's this wind, blowing and blowing, and that the weather today could have changed like this, it was so calm and brown and slow enough earlier today, but now the wind is blowing and it's raining, like something evil, she thinks, and if he could just come home now, this waiting, always this waiting, she must like it, she must like to wait, she thinks and she sees, lying there on the bench, herself walk across the room, to the hall door, and she sees herself stop there, stand there in the middle of the room and stare emptily into space, and this, that she always sees herself, she thinks, she can hardly do anything else, that everything that was should still be there, exactly as it was, yes, yes, it doesn't help to think about it, she thinks and then she sees him before her, how he came walking up to her, the slightly bent way he walks, the long black hair, suddenly he was just there, just stood there, and it was as though he had always been there, and now, and, yes, ever since then that was just how it was, and there was nothing to do about it, it was as though there was no way to get away from it, because she's tried, of course, she's tried, she thought this and thought that, did this and did that, and no matter what she did or didn't do it was still more and more just the two of them, as though there was nothing the will could do, and the same with him, he also wanted and didn't want, he tried as much as he could to get free of it but then, yes, then everything stayed how it was and how it had always been, she

48

thinks, and she can't just stay lying here like this, she thinks, she has to get up, stand up, she has to do something, she can't just stay lying here on the bench, she thinks and she sees herself standing there in the room and looking emptily into space and then she sees herself go over to the hall door and she sees herself take hold of the door handle and she sees herself stand there with her hand on the door handle and she thinks, standing there holding the door handle, why hasn't he come home? and always the same thing, waiting, waiting, but he's been gone such a long time, can't he come soon, she thinks and she lets go of the door handle and she sees, lying there on the bench, herself go over to the window again and she sees herself stop and then she's standing there again and looking out the window and she thinks that now he really has to come home soon and he thinks damn, the water is so rough now, and damn, the tide is so high, he thinks standing there on the pier, the weather is as terrible as it can be, he thinks, the tide is high, so high that whenever a wave came in it crashed over the pier and up over his boots, and his boat is rocking up and down out there in the waves, so high that it seems like the boat will tip over, it tips up so high and then so far down that it seems like the next wave will crash in over the bow and fill the boat, it goes so far down, before it goes up again, and again, and yet again, but if the water gets much rougher now then he doesn't see how it could turn out all right, he thinks and he turns around and he thinks that he'd better just go back home, there's nothing he can do about it anyway, he thinks, but the weather isn't really that bad, is it? it's windy, that's true, but does that really matter? and the boat sure is good, it would hold up well even in this weather, he thinks, so maybe he should go out onto the fjord for a while today too, because the boat is good, yes, he thinks, it would stand up to these waves too, he thinks, yes why not? why shouldn't he go out for a while? he thinks and he walks out to the end of the pier and the waves crash up over his boots and he unties the mooring lines and he starts to pull the boat in, just a little while, he needs just a little while out in the waves and in the wind and in the rain, and in the darkness, he thinks and he needs to be careful, so that the boat doesn't crash against the pier, he thinks and he carefully pulls the boat in and then he grabs hold of the stern with one hand and puts one foot down in the bow and then the next foot and then he is on board and the waves rock him and the boat up and down and he shoves off and he takes an oar in his hands and he pushes the oar against the pier and he shoves off and he unties the stern line and up and down rocks the boat there in the darkness and he sits down on the middle seat and he puts out the oars and he rows as hard as he can against the waves and it goes well, the boat goes up and down in the waves, and he rows as hard as he can and the boat starts moving forwards, sluggishly, quietly, slowly, up and down, there in the waves, up and down, but forwards, it's moving, and the boat moves out across the fjord, out further and further, in the wind, in the rain, and even though the darkness is dense and thick around him in a weird way it's not dark, he thinks, because the fjord is shining black and then it's not really that cold, he is wearing his thick black sweater after all, and he is keeping warm from rowing, he thinks and he looks back over his shoulder and there, up ahead, far away there, there near the middle of the fjord, what is that over there? doesn't it look like a fire? but it, no it can't be! he thinks and he rests on the oars and right away the waves carry him so fast towards land that he starts to row again and he looks back over his shoulder and there and yes he is sure of it, he thinks, that's a fire there, it looks like a fire in any case and a big fire too, and yes yes, yes, it's burning out there, there in the middle of the fjord, he thinks and he keeps rowing and he looks in towards shore and there, there up on the shore there, there, isn't that Grandma standing there? isn't Grandma standing there and looking out across the fjord? no really, really! he thinks, no he doesn't understand anything, he thinks, and he sets to his oars, and now he'll just row over to where this thing like a fire is, he thinks, and now she is surely standing there in front of the window waiting for him and he thinks that he loves her so much and she thinks that now she really does have to go look for him, she thinks, standing there in front of the window and looking out into the darkness, and that she's just like that, she just has to stand here in front of the window all the time, she thinks and she looks out into the darkness and she sees a fire, there in the middle of the fjord, a pale purple fire, there's a pale purple fire out there in the middle of the darkness there out on the fjord now, she thinks and she sees the rain running down over the windowpane and he's staying out so long, she thinks, and she really does need to go look for him? she thinks, now she really needs to go out, she needs to go look for him? she thinks, because why hasn't he come home yet? he doesn't usually stay out on the water so long? well, yes, he does, a lot, yes, it's happened pretty often, so then why is she hanging around worrying? nothing is out of the ordinary, everything is the same as always, there's nothing special about today, she thinks, but still it's strange, and what is she supposed to do if he doesn't come home? she could just go look for him, she thinks, go down to the boathouse, to the pier, but the weather is just so nasty outside, it's raining and the wind is blowing and it's late in the autumn, a day in late November, and it's cold, it's a

Tuesday in late November, and he'll be home soon enough, she's just worrying, she thinks, but, yes, she knows herself, no, now she has to just pull herself together, she thinks, everything is the way it should be, and he'll be home soon enough now, she thinks, she's just worrying, it's just, it's, no, she thinks, and she can't just stay standing like that, she can just go out, go down to the fjord and look for him, she thinks and she sees, lying there on the bench, herself go over to the hall door and she opens it and at the moment the door opens and she sees herself go out she sees a boy come in and she sees the door shut again and then she sees the boy go over to the window and stop and then he stands there and looks out the window and the boy must be six or seven years old, she thinks, he's a little kid, she thinks and then she sees the hall door open and a man, tall and thin, and lanky, and with long black hair, and a thin black beard, comes in and then he stands there and he looks sort of pretend-strict and he holds one hand behind his back and then a woman comes in, short, dark, thin, with long black hair, she looks a little like she herself looks, and she shuts the door again after her and the man with the beard winks at the woman and the man and the woman both look at the boy and he turns around to face them, and he looks at them with such big eyes, and they both smile at him

Asle, the woman says then

I think Daddy has something for you, because you're seven years old today, it's your seventh birthday, 17 November, she says

17 November 1897, that's today's date, just like Brita says, Kristoffer says

and Asle looks at the two of them, so eager, so shy

It certainly is, yes, just like Brita says, Kristoffer says

and Kristoffer puts his free arm around Brita's shoulders and then Kristoffer suddenly takes his other hand out from behind his back and in his hand there's a boat, a little rowboat, one or two feet long, and with seats and oars and bailers and everything a boat should have, and he holds out the boat to Asle

Happy birthday, Asle, you're seven, Kristoffer says

A big boy like you needs his own boat, a good boy like you, Asle, he says

Yes you're such a good boy Asle, Brita says

and Asle goes over to Kristoffer, who is holding the boat out to him, and Asle takes the boat, and he stands there and looks at it, and then Kristoffer puts out his hand and Asle takes his hand and then Kristoffer shakes hands with Asle in a slow movement up and down and Asle just stands there and looks and looks at the boat

That's a nice boat, Kristoffer says

You can see it has seats and floorboards and oars and bailers and everything, he says

And it's so white and such nice woodwork, and the boat smells a little of tar, just like a brand-new boat should smell, Brita says

That's a nice boat Kristoffer built for you, she says

It's because you are such a handsome little man Asle, Kristoffer says

You built it, Asle says

and Kristoffer says yes he did build it, because when he was young, a long time ago, he studied with a boat-builder, and even if he didn't build that many boats with him he did learn how to build boats, yes, he says and then Kristoffer goes over to Asle, who is looking and looking at the boat, and Kristoffer puts his arms around Asle's shoulders

I have to go try out the boat right now, Asle says

Yes, the waves probably aren't too high, Kristoffer says

But be careful now, Brita says

Yes, you have to be careful, she says

Asle is careful, you know he is, Kristoffer says

and Asle stands there and looks and looks at the boat and then he goes out the hall door and Kristoffer nods to Brita and she smiles at him and then she sees, lying there on the bench, Brita go through the door to the kitchen and Kristoffer go through it after her and shut the door after him and then she sees herself come in through the open hall door with a raincoat on and she sees herself stop in the doorway and look into the room and then she sees herself go out and shut the door after her and she thinks, standing there in the hall, that now, no, she can't remember him ever being this late before, it's almost nighttime and he hasn't come home, she has to go look for him, she has to go down to the boathouse, to the pier, she has to go look for him, because this, this wind, this rain, this darkness, and can't he come home soon, she thinks and she goes out the front door and the wind is blowing, it's raining, and the darkness is black, and it's so cold, and she has to lean against the front door to get it closed, the wind is blowing so hard, and she leans against it, gets the door closed, and then she is standing there in the light outside, on the front step, and she hears the waves, the rain, and then the waves, and it's so cold, and she can't just stay standing like that, she thinks, since she went out in the first place because she wanted to go down to the shore and look for him, maybe call his name, but she can't just stand there in the evening darkness and call his name? can she? no she probably can't do that, she can't, no, she thinks and she goes out into the yard and she goes around the corner, stops and stands there and looks down the little road, and isn't that him coming walking up the little road, in this black darkness she can see him, she really can, no, that's good, she thinks, but there, on the little road, no that isn't him who's coming, it's a woman coming, hurrying, and she's carrying a child in her arms, and the child is so big in her arms, no what is this? she thinks, what's happening? and she can see everything so clearly, as though it was the middle of the day, no she doesn't understand this, she thinks and she sees the woman come hurrying towards her and she really is carrying a boy in her arms and she's pressing the boy to her chest, and the woman is going so fast, and the boy, is he alive? because the woman who's coming towards her is carrying a boy in her arms and the boy looks lifeless, his clothes are wet, his hair is wet, and in the woman's eyes, her big eyes, there is something like a yellow sunbeam of despair, but what's going on, what is this? she thinks and the woman, she has thick black long hair, stops there on the little road and then she stands there and presses the boy to her chest and the woman just stands there, in the middle of the little road, head bent, with a boy in her arms, and she looks at the woman, who's standing there, completely motionless, and then she hears a voice call out what is it? and she looks down at the fjord and there, on the path to the boat-house, she sees a man, tall and slim, lanky, and with long black hair, with a thin black beard, come running up the hill and he has a string with fish on it in one hand and one side of his long hair has fallen in front of his face

What is it Brita? the man calls out

What's happened, what's wrong with Asle, he calls out

and the man runs up and she sees that Brita's black hair, her thick black hair, is hanging down and covering Asle the boy she is holding in her arms and then Brita starts to rock herself and Asle back and forth and the man is in front of Brita and Asle and then he stands there and puts his arms around them and behind Asle's back the fish that the man has on the string hang down to the ground and the man's long black hair falls down over Brita's hair and down over Asle and they just stand there, motionless, while time just passes, she thinks, they stand there, just stand there, and Kristoffer lets go of Brita, goes a little way away from her

What happened? he says

Asle fell in the water, Brita says

Is he still alive, the man says

Yes Kristoffer, Brita says

It's his seventh birthday, it's Asle's seventh birthday, Kristoffer says

Asle's dead, Brita, he says

No he's not dead, you can't say that, don't say that Kristoffer, Brita says

Asle's dead, Kristoffer says

He turned seven years old and then he died, he says

No he's still alive, Brita says

Look, don't you see, he's dead, Kristoffer says

and Brita stands there with Asle in her arms and Asle's arms hang straight down, and his head hangs down, and his eyes are open and empty

You weren't grown up yet, you were just seven, you should have lived such a long life, not a short one like this, Kristoffer says

and Brita stands there, bent forwards, with her long thick black hair hanging down over Asle

He's still alive, Brita says

and Brita looks up through her hair at Kristoffer

No he's dead, Kristoffer says

and Kristoffer goes a little further away from Brita, and he stops, looks at her

Brita, Kristoffer says

and Brita doesn't answer, just stays standing there like

before, with that long black hair hanging down over her eyes

Asle is dead, Kristoffer says

Asle's alive, Brita says

Don't say that, Kristoffer, don't say that he's dead, she says

Asle's gone, Kristoffer says

He's dead, he says

and Kristoffer starts to walk up the little road, he goes around the corner, he walks across the yard, slowly, step by step, and the fish on the string swing from side to side, and it is as if Kristoffer will collapse before he takes half a step and turn into the earth that he walks on, she thinks and she sees Kristoffer stop and stand and look down, he stands there with a string with fish on it in one hand and he looks down and she turns around and then she starts to go down the little road and she stops next to Brita and then she lifts her hand and then she lightly smoothes down Brita's hair, she strokes and strokes and smoothes down her hair and then she hears footsteps and then she sees Kristoffer come walking down the little road and the fish on the string are swinging from side to side and Kristoffer stops too and then he also smoothes down Brita's hair

Come inside now, Brita, Kristoffer says

You can't just stand here, he says

We have to go inside, he says

We have to take Asle inside, he says

and Brita looks up and through her long hair she looks at Kristoffer

It's 17 November today, Brita says

17 November 1897, Kristoffer says

17 November 1897, Brita says

and Kristoffer puts his arm around Brita's shoulders

and Kristoffer and Brita, and Brita with Asle in her arms, slowly walk up the little road

On 17 November 1897, Asle died, Brita says

And he was born on 17 November 1890, she says

and Kristoffer stops, and Brita stops, and then they stand there and look down at the brown earth and then the front door of the old house opens and an old woman comes out and stops on the front step and Kristoffer looks at her

He's gone, Asle's gone, Old Aliss, Kristoffer says

Don't just stand there like that, Old Aliss says

The Lord moves in mysterious ways, she says

He is happy, Asle's happy now with God in Heaven, so don't be sad, she says

Don't be sad, she says

God is good, He is, she says

and Old Aliss lifts one hand, with its stubby bent fingers, up to her eye and she rubs along the edge of her eye with the side of her finger

God is good, she says

and then Old Aliss bends her head and a shudder goes through her shoulders and then she just stands there, she just stands, the way Kristoffer and Brita are just standing there too, and Brita with Asle in her arms. It gets darker and darker, and they are just standing there. They just stand there, they just don't move, she thinks. They stand there, they stand there as though they had been standing there since time immemorial, she thinks. And she stands there. She stands there and looks at Asle, at Brita, Kristoffer, Old Aliss. And then she turns around and far away, up on the ridge, where the farmsteads end before it slopes down to the river on the other side, the river that follows the back of the ridge all the way from the waterfall further back, there, up on the very top of the ridge, she sees a boy standing there, he stands there completely calm, just stands, and he looks down at the old house where they live, and isn't that a stick in his hand? yes, it is, a long stick cut from a branch is resting on his shoulder, and maybe he's been fishing in the river with the stick? she thinks and then she sees the boy, and could it be him as a boy? doesn't it look like him? but how could she even tell from such a great distance that it's him? she thinks, but she can because he is both very far away and right up close, and because it is as if it's totally dark and totally light at the same time, she thinks, and she can't understand it, because she can see a boy far away standing up at the top of the ridge, and she can also see his face perfectly clearly as though he was right next to her, and now she sees so so clearly that it's him and she sees him start to run towards her, and then suddenly it's a different face, a totally different face, but still with black hair, like his black hair, and doesn't it look like the Asle that Brita is standing and holding in her arms now? she thinks, yes it really does, she thinks and she sees the boy run towards her, but isn't it him as a boy? yes now it's him again, and not the Asle that Brita is standing with in her arms, now she can see it so clearly, and then, it wasn't him before, it was someone else, a boy the same age, but a different boy, and this boy is probably the Asle that Brita is standing and holding in her arms, and now the boy comes almost right up to the yard and she turns around and she looks at the old house where they live and there, in the yard, she sees Brita still standing with Asle in her arms and Kristoffer stands there with the fish on the string and Old Aliss stands on the front step and now she sees it, now she sees it, now she sees that the boy who is coming running towards her is the Asle that Brita is standing with in her arms and she sees the boy drop the stick and then it is as if he disappears into the boy Brita is standing and holding in her arms. And then Old Aliss straightens up, standing there on the front step, and she slowly turns around and goes into the old house. Into her house, Old Aliss goes into her house, she thinks. And in the yard in front of the old house where they live Brita stands holding Asle in her arms. And then Kristoffer goes over to Brita and then he takes Asle into his own arms and then he hugs Asle to his body, and the string with the fish hangs and swings down towards the ground, and then Kristoffer starts to rock himself and Asle back and forth, and the fish on the string swing back and forth

No he can't be dead, Brita says

and Kristoffer doesn't answer

My good little boy can't have left us, she says

My son, my darling son, she says

My dearest son, she says

But where is Olaf, she says

Do you know where Olaf is, Kristoffer, she says

and as though he was carrying Asle to his baptism Kristoffer goes into the old house where they live and Brita stays standing and then Brita runs her hand through her hair so that it falls back from her forehead and her face is there like an empty sky and then Brita goes home into the old house, where she lives herself, into the old house where she has lived with him for years and years now, into her house, Brita goes into the house that became her own house, she thinks, she is going in to where she is, in her strange clothes and with her long thick black hair Brita is going into her house, into the old house that's hers and his, she thinks, and so, if someone else has gone into her house, if someone else lives in the old house, then she herself probably can't go in? if it's not her house any more? and so can she go inside it? she thinks, no she probably can't? but it's she and he who live there, no one else lives there, she thinks, they have lived there for years and years, the two of them, just the two of them, she thinks and then she notices the rain, she is standing outside after all, in the rain, in the darkness, and the wind is blowing, and it's cold, and she can't just stay standing here outside, she thinks, but he hasn't come home. And where is he? Where has he gone? He must have gone out onto the fjord in his boat, but he still hasn't come back, and she's really worried about him, can something have happened to him? she thinks, why doesn't he come back? but she thinks things like that all the time, she thinks, almost every day, because every day he rows out in his boat, he does, and she is almost always worried about him and thinks that now he really needs to come home, she thinks. And is today any different? Probably not, as far as she knows, she thinks. Everything is probably the same as always. Everything is the same as always. It's an ordinary Tuesday in late November, 1979. And she is she. And he is he. But maybe she should still go down to the shore, go down to the boathouse, maybe she should still go look for him all the same? she thinks. Yes that's what she'll do, she thinks. It's good to get outside for a few minutes, even if it is windy and raining, she thinks. It's refreshing. She can't just stay inside at home all the time. She spends much too much time indoors. Whole days, she often doesn't set foot outside all day. No it's not good. She needs to get out of the house too, every once in a while. And hanging around worrying like that, isn't that pretty much what she does all the time? yes, well, but anyway she can still go down to the fjord, she thinks, she could surely do that, she thinks, and in any case why does she just stay standing here? if she wants to go she should go, she can't stay standing here, she thinks, it's a Tuesday in late November, 1979, and she is just standing there, she thinks, and then she starts to walk down the little road, but just now, wasn't that him she had seen coming up the road? no it can't have been him, it was probably just something she imagined, she thinks, but now she has to go down to the shore and look for him, it's raining, it's windy, and it's got so dark now, it's got so dark that she can hardly see to walk, and this, this frightful weather, and this cold, and why would he row out in a boat when the weather's like this? she thinks, why would he do that? no, she doesn't understand it, why doesn't he want to stay with her? she thinks, instead he always rows out in that boat, that little boat, a little row-boat, and now he has to come home, she thinks, and she has got so worried, because he never stays out on the fjord so long, not in weather like this, and when it's so dark, and so cold, she can't remember him ever staying out so long before, and why doesn't he come home? what's wrong? and nothing bad can have happened, can it? she thinks, and maybe he'll never come back? no she can't think like that, she thinks, now she really does have to just go down to the shore, and she can just stand there on the pier for a while and look for him, because then, if she stands there, it might just happen that he'll come back sooner, she thinks, because she's done that lots of times before, yes, lots of times, really a lot, she's gone down to the boat-house and the pier for a while, down to look for him, she has stood there so many times on the pier and waited for him to come back to shore, it's probably the evening walk she takes most often, that, she thinks and she crosses the big road and she goes down the path and then she hears a woman call out Asle, Asle and she goes around the corner of the boathouse and she stops and there on the shore she sees that long thick hair of Brita's and she hears Brita again calling Asle, Asle! and then she sees a little boat, one

62

or two feet long, a pretty little rowboat, lying there floating in the black water and then she sees Asle's head come
up out of the fjord and she sees that his hands are flailing
there in the waves and then she sees Brita run out onto the
pier and Asle's head disappears again under the water, his
hands, all of him disappears under the water and then his
boat is lying there and floating and being pulled further
out into the fjord and Brita jumps off the pier and starts to
swim out into the fjord and the boat disappears behind a
wave and Brita tries to swim as hard as she can, she fights,
struggles forwards, against the waves, and the waves push
her back and Brita shouts Asle! Asle! there between the
waves and she can see Asle's head again, coming up there
between two waves

Asle! Brita shouts

and she hears that Brita's scream fills everything there
is, the fjord, the mountain, and Asle doesn't answer, and
then a big wave comes and washes over Asle and capsizes
his boat and then it's lying there and tossing in the water
and bumping against Brita and then she can't see Asle's
head any more and Brita grabs hold of his hair and she
holds it tight and the waves hit them and Brita's free hand
hits the fjord and hits and hits and a big wave carries Brita
and Asle in towards shore and then Brita is standing up
a little on the underwater slope there and a wave crash-
es over her head and she walks heavily in onto the shore
and pulls Asle with her by the hair and only his head is
above water and then Brita comes more and more out of
the water and her hair is hanging long and black down
over her face, and then Asle's upper body is above water, and Brita pulls Asle toward her and she puts one arm
under his knee and the other behind his back, and Brita
picks Asle up and with her face turned toward the rain
Brita wades in onto the shore with Asle in her arms and

his hands hang straight down and Brita reaches the shore and with Asle in her arms Brita starts to go up to the boathouse and she sees that Brita with Asle in her arms goes around the corner of the boathouse and then she sees Asle's boat lying there floating so pretty in the water and she sees Asle standing there holding a stick and there is a thin line going from the stick to his boat and Asle walks along the shore and he pulls the boat carefully along with the stick and the boat is so shining and it moves so gently over the water and then he stops pulling on the stick and lets the boat glide along and then his boat is lying there and rising and falling up and down in the fjord and then Asle raises the stick and the boat makes a slow curve and then the boat glides in towards the shore and then Asle walks backwards a little and then he guides the boat into a kind of cove he has made between two big stones and then he puts down the stick and then Asle starts to put mussel shells into the boat, one blue mussel shell after another, and fills up the whole boat, and then Asle gives the boat a little shove and it moves out from his bay between the two stones, and then he takes the stick and he starts to walk further along the shore and the boat slides so slowly and steadily along and the blazing motionless water comes almost up to the edge of the boat and Asle guides the boat calmly along and then Asle turns around and he sees Kristoffer come into view around the corner of the boathouse

So, Asle, what kind of cargo are you carrying today, Kristoffer says

I'm taking my shipment to Bergen, Asle says

What kind of shipment, Kristoffer says

Different things, Asle says

You don't want to tell, Kristoffer says

Mm no, Asle says

and Kristoffer says that's all right, confidential trade secrets, everyone needs a few of those, he says and he asks if he'll be staying a long time in Bergen

A few days, Asle says

Yes well once you've sailed to the city, why not, Kristoffer says

The trip takes a whole day, it, yes it does, Asle says

That's true, Kristoffer says

and Kristoffer walks out onto the pier and he starts to pull his boat in towards him

Are you going out in the boat, Asle says

I'm going to do a little fishing, we need food after all, Kristoffer says

Can I go with you, Asle says

Sure you can, Kristoffer says

No never mind, Asle says

I don't have time for that, he says

Yes I can certainly understand that, Kristoffer says

You have a full cargo and you were on your way to Bergen, weren't you, he says

I'll go with you later, another time, Asle says

Yes, you're sailing to Bergen, aren't you now, Kristoffer says

Yes I am, Asle says

and then Kristoffer's boat comes up to the pier, and Kristoffer climbs on board, unties the mooring lines, sits down on the seat, puts the oars in the water, and rows a little way out into the bay, then he stops there and rests on his oars

Talk to you later, when you get back from Bergen, Kristoffer says

OK, Asle says

And you'll bring back some treats with you, right, Kristoffer says

I can probably do that, Asle says

and then Kristoffer puts the oars down into the water and rows out into the fjord and Asle goes further along the shore and his boat moves so prettily along and Kristoffer rows with strong strokes and his boat disappears back behind the headland and then the water ripples and some little waves make Asle's boat roll from side to side and Asle lifts up the stick, and the front of the boat is hanging in the air above the water, and the back of the boat is down in the water, and then the mussel shells slide back out of the boat and fall into the water and Asle pulls hard on the stick and then the line comes loose from the fitting on the boat and then his boat stays lying there and drifting without a mooring line and Asle tries to reach it with the stick and just barely does it, he reaches the boat and he carefully tries to make it come closer to shore, he pushes lightly against it with the stick, and then he slips and the boat shoots off to the side out into the fjord and Asle puts down the stick, finds himself a stone, throws it, and the stone hits the water right in front of the boat and the waves from the stone push the boat further from land and Asle finds himself another stone and he throws it and this time it hits the outside of the boat and it comes closer to shore again and Asle picks up the stick, gets hold of the boat with it, and he guides the boat in onto the shore. And Asle picks up the boat. And Asle stands there with the boat in his hands and looks at it and then he puts the boat down in the fjord again, and then the boat is lying there in the bay between the two stones and Asle finds some twigs, breaks some pieces off an old plank of wood that's lying there, loads the boat up well, and then Asle takes the boat in his hands and then he pushes it out a ways and the boat glides out so prettily and Asle finds a little stone, throws it behind the boat, and the boat is pushed further out by the waves the stone makes, it bobs up and down, bobs up, bobs down, and then Asle finds a bunch of stones and he throws them one after another behind the boat and it glides further and further out onto the fjord and soon the boat is a long way out in the bay and it glides slowly further out onto the fjord and Asle finds a big and very heavy stone, he takes the stone in his hands and he manages to pick it up and he carries the stone down to the edge of the water and he takes the stone in one hand and tries to lift it up behind his head, but he can't do it, and he holds the stone with both hands and holds it as far out to one side as he can and he throws it and the stone splashes into the water just a little ways out and the stone makes big waves that splash water both in onto him and out onto the boat and the boat shoots out onto the bay and Asle sees the boat glide further and further out onto the fjord and then it's as if the weather has suddenly changed, it gets dark, the wind starts to blow, it rains, the waves come in and the boat bobs up and down and goes further and further out onto the fjord and then Asle kicks off his wooden shoes and he unbuttons his pants and pulls them off and then he walks out into the water, he is standing in water up to his knees, and then a wave comes almost up to his waist and there far away out there is his boat and he looks at the boat and she sees, standing there on the shore, Asle wade out and she sees him disappear under the water and she thinks that now he really does need to come back soon and she goes out onto the pier and it's so dark that she can't see anything, and now he has to come soon, she thinks, and then this wind, and this darkness, and the waves, the high tide, and it's so cold, and the water is so rough that the waves are crashing over the pier all the way up to her, it's horrible weather, she thinks, and now he really does need to come back soon, she thinks, and out there? isn't that something like a light out there? like firelight, out in the middle of the fjord there? and doesn't it look purple? no there can't be anything like that out there, but still, she thinks, and where is he? and his boat? she can't see anything, but where is he? and why doesn't he come back? doesn't he want to be with her? is that why? and to think that anyone would want to be out on the fjord in weather like this, and in this darkness, no she just doesn't understand, she thinks and she tries to see out across the fjord, but she can't see anything, and now he really does have to come soon, she thinks, he really can't stay out on the fjord in weather like this, in darkness like this, in this weather, and in that little boat, a little rowboat, she thinks. And then this darkness. And it's so cold. And can she just stand here? But why doesn't he come? And can she even remember him ever being out in weather like this before, and so late in the evening? she thinks, no, nothing comes to mind, well, or maybe he has? no she doesn't believe he has, he probably never has, she thinks, and now she can't just stand here like this, she thinks, because she's freezing, it's cold, and can she call his name? no she can't, she probably can't just call his name? that wouldn't work to stand here in the darkness and call his name, she thinks, but what should she do? someone has to look for him! yes! someone has to find him! but who? she has to go get someone with a big boat with a good light to row out onto the fjord and find him, she thinks, but who? does she know anyone? no she really doesn't know anyone who could do that, she thinks, so she just has to stand here, stay standing here, she really has to just stay standing here waiting, she thinks, and what else? call his name? find someone with a big boat? a big boat with a light? or just wait? stand here and wait? or go home and wait? just go back home and wait? because she can't stay here, and she's sure he's coming home soon, he's probably just out a little late, she thinks and she walks back in along the pier and she stops, because there, there far away on the shore, there's a fire burning, and can it be a Midsummer's Day fire? and aren't those two boys standing there around the fire? yes, she's sure of it, yes, and they're not the boys from the neighbouring farm, are they? she thinks, yes it must be the two neighbour boys, but a fire? and now, at this time of year? in this weather? no it can't be, she thinks, no one would build a fire in this weather, no, no one could probably even start a fire on an evening like this, but there it is, a fire is burning on the shore and two boys around ten or twelve years old are standing and looking at the fire and isn't that something like a boat, a rowboat, that's burning? isn't that a boat just like the one he had? she thinks, no, that's strange, she thinks and she looks at the flames rising up from the boat, they've set fire to the boat in different places and the fire has the shape of a boat and then they're standing around it these two boys and they're staring into the flames, and what is this? she thinks, no she doesn't understand, it can't be, she thinks and she can't stay standing here on the pier, because it's cold, and she's freezing, and this rain, this wind, but he, he's not coming soon? what's happened to him? she thinks and she starts to walk back in along the pier again, and then there's that strange fire, she thinks, a boat burning far away down on the shore, and two boys standing and looking and looking at the burning boat, no really what is this? she thinks, and now, at this time of year, why? she thinks and she goes around the corner of the boathouse and she walks up the path and now the rain and the wind have got stronger and the darkness is so dense and thick now that she can't see her own feet, and now she has to get indoors, get into the house, she thinks, now she has to go back to the old house where they live and tend the fire, because it can't go out in the stove, when he comes back from the fjord wet and icy it has to be warm in the house, at home in the old house, in the fine old room at home in the old house, where they live, where they've lived for years and years now, she thinks, now she has to get home, and has to make sure there's a lot of wood in the stove, she thinks and she walks up the little road and she stops and she turns around, because didn't she hear something behind her? footsteps? she heard something, she thinks and she looks down at the shore and a fire is still burning there, but it's not as big as before, now the fire is like there were only a few planks of wood burning, and it burns weakly, and that a fire should be burning down there on the shore now, in the dark evening, in this rain, in this wind, she thinks and she looks at the fire going out, and everything becomes dark and then a single flame flares up, then everything turns back into darkness, then a single flame flares up again, but now it's smaller, and then everything turns back into darkness and then a single flame flares up one more time but it's so small that it can only barely be seen, and then it's dark. Just dark. Just the rain. And just the wind. And now she really does need to get indoors, she thinks and she goes around the corner of the old house where they live and there in front of her in the yard she sees an old woman walking in a blue coat, and on her head she has on the yellow-white cap that he always wears, and the old woman supports herself with a walking stick, and she walks slowly forwards and in one hand she's holding a red shopping bag, and then she sees that there's a little boy walking along with the old woman and he is holding one handle of the shopping bag too, and now she sees it, because it's him as a boy! it's him walking there, she thinks and she sees that the old woman has put two crooked fingers on his little hand and the old woman and he go up to the front step and she leans the walking stick against the wall and opens the front door

So now we better go in the house, let's go in, Asle and Grandma, Grandma says

Yes let's go in, Asle says

You were such a good boy, Asle, to help Grandma so much with her bag, Grandma says

After Grandpa Olaf died, you've been my biggest help, she says

and she sees Grandma go in the front door and he goes in after her and she thinks that no, she can't just stay standing out here in the cold even if someone else has just gone into her house, home into the old house, because it is her house after all, it's she and he who live there, she thinks, and besides it was definitely him who went inside just now, and the old woman, that was his Grandma, she thinks, so then, so, then maybe she can still just go in? she thinks, and she really does need to just go inside, she too, because it's windy and raining too much for her to be able to stay standing here outside, this wind, this rain, and this cold, she needs to get indoors too, she thinks, but can she really go home into the old house when someone else lives there? she thinks, but really it's she who lives there, they who live there, she and he, Signe and Asle, so she just has to go in, she thinks and she goes in and there in the hall she sees Grandma stand and take off her yellow-white hat and she puts it on the shelf and then Grandma unbuttons her coat and she takes it off and hangs it on a peg

Can you shut the front door, Asle, Grandma says

and she looks at him going and shutting the front door

Yes, it's cold these days, Asle, so we can't let the warmth get out, Grandma says

And it's slippery, it's dangerous for an old woman like Grandma to walk out there, yes, even just stepping outside, she says

But for you, for you it's not dangerous, you're young, Asle, she says

No not for me, Asle says

Not for you, no, you're young, Grandma says

and she sees that Grandma takes hold of her red shopping bag and opens the door to the kitchen and goes in and then she sees that he goes in after her and shuts the door behind him and now she just has to go inside and lay more wood in the stove, she thinks, because it needs to be warm in the house when he comes home, now she has to just go inside and then she has to fill up the stove well, she thinks, because it can't go out, it has to be nice and warm in the room when he comes home from the water, with the wind blowing like this, with it raining like this, it's so dark out there, and so cold, so when he comes home it has to be warm and nice in the room here at home in the old house, she thinks and she takes off her raincoat and she hangs it up on the peg where Grandma just hung up her coat, she hangs her raincoat over Grandma's coat, and then she goes over to the door to the room and she opens it and she goes in and she sees, lying there on the bench, herself come into the room and she sees herself turn around and go and shut the door and then she sees herself go over to the woodbox and take out a couple logs and she sees herself bend down and put the logs into the stove and then she sees herself stand up there on the floor in the room and stand there and look at the flames and she thinks, standing there, that it's good that it didn't go out, that it's still burning, and here inside it isn't so cold, so if he could just come home now, she thinks and then she sees the kitchen door open and then the smell of bacon glides into the room and then she sees him come in from the kitchen and right after him comes Grandma

Just sit down at the table, the food's almost ready, Grandma says

You're so nice, Grandma, Asle says

You're such a good boy, Asle, Grandma says

We are good friends, the two of us, aren't we, Asle says

and she sees him go over to the table and he sits down at the end of the table and she sees him sit there and swing his legs back and forth and Grandma goes out to the kitchen again and he sits there and swings his legs back and forth and then Grandma comes in with a plate of bacon and eggs, and roasted potatoes and fried onions, and in her other hand Grandma has a big glass of milk

Yes now you'll have some good hearty food, Grandma says

and Grandma puts the plate and the glass down in front of him and he starts to eat and Grandma sits down at the other end of the table and she, lying there on the bench, sees herself standing and looking at the flames in the stove and then she sees herself go over to the window and she sees herself stand there and look out the window and then she looks, standing there in front of the window, at the bedroom door and it opens and then she sees Brita stand and hold the door open and she sees her hair clinging tight around her face and then she sees Kristoffer standing in the bedroom door and in his arms he is holding a little white wooden coffin and he walks into the room

So, it has to be, Kristoffer says

Yes we have to say farewell, Brita says

It has to be, Kristoffer says

and she sees Brita shut the bedroom door and then Brita opens the hall door and stands there and holds it open and she sees that Old Aliss is standing out there in the hall and tears are running down over her unsteady face and then she sees Kristoffer walk out the door with the little white wooden coffin in his arms and then Brita walks out, shuts the door behind her and then she sees, lying there on the bench, herself go over to the bench and then she sees herself lie down on the bench and she puts her hands up under her sweater and up to her breasts and then she lies there and holds her breasts and then she pulls up her skirt with one hand and she pulls her hand up over her thigh and she puts her hand in between her legs, she lets her hand lie there, and she looks at the table and she sees him stand up

Thanks for the food Grandma, Asle says

Yes good, Grandma says

and Grandma stands up, takes his plate and he takes the empty glass

That was really good, Asle says

Thank you, Asle, Grandma says

and then Grandma goes out to the kitchen and he goes after her and he shuts the door behind him and then they are gone, gone forever, she thinks lying there on the bench and she thinks that today, today it's probably Thursday, and it's March, and the year is 2002, she thinks and she looks at the bedroom door and it opens and then he's standing there

Don't you want to come to bed soon, he says

I've warmed up the bed, he says

and he pushes his long black hair back behind his ears, and he looks at her

You need to come to bed too, come soon, he says

and she looks at him and then she looks away from him into the emptiness and then she lays both her hands on her stomach and she folds her hands and I hear Signe say

Dear Jesus, help me, you have to help me, you

Translator's Note

The Norwegian title of this novel is *Det er Ales*, which means 'That's Ales' or 'It's Ales'; the woman's name in the original is Ales, not Aliss. Unfortunately, this Norwegian name coincides with the English word for a type of beer, and would certainly be interpreted that way in a title without other context: *It's Ales* would come across as a very different book than the one Fosse wrote. Since publishing this book in 2004, Fosse has written a *Trilogy* and *Septology* with multiple characters named Asle and Ales, so the decision might have been different now, but a dozen years ago I decided I needed to change Ales's name and the book's title. This second edition follows the first English translation, published in 2010, but readers should know that Aliss is another one of Fosse's characters named Ales.

Back then I emailed Fosse to ask what the name Ales meant to him and what he wanted the title to convey. I had noticed that the book's first burst of short sentences, after forty or so pages flowing by without a full stop, included the sentence 'Det er Ales,' so the title should refer to that moment in the book, but what else? Fosse told me that Ales was a very old-fashioned name, 'maybe your grandmother might have known an old woman named Ales'. He himself had a great-great-grandmother named Ales who was known as a 'wise woman', a healer. She really did heal people, and the sick came to see her from far and wide; at one point she was called in to see the local priest, to talk about her 'practice', but there was no punishment. About the title, Fosse said: 'It means Ales is spreading out over the whole universe.'

I love these answers – they are like how I imagine a genius director doesn't tell actors what to do, just offers some comment that makes the actors realize they already know. I realized the character's name should be recognizably a name but unusual, mysterious, with a certain aura – not contemporary like Alice or Alissa. (*That's Alice* would also evoke *Go Ask Alice* or *Alice in Wonderland*, which would be unfortunate associations). And the title should be something archetypal: the most universal moment or image from that burst of short sentences.

I am grateful for all of Fosse's help, and his continuing trust in me; I would also like to thank Mari Jahrsengene and Grethe Fatima Syéd for their assistance with the 2010 translation.

Minneapolis, July 2022

This translation has been published with the financial support of NORLA, Norwegian Literature Abroad.